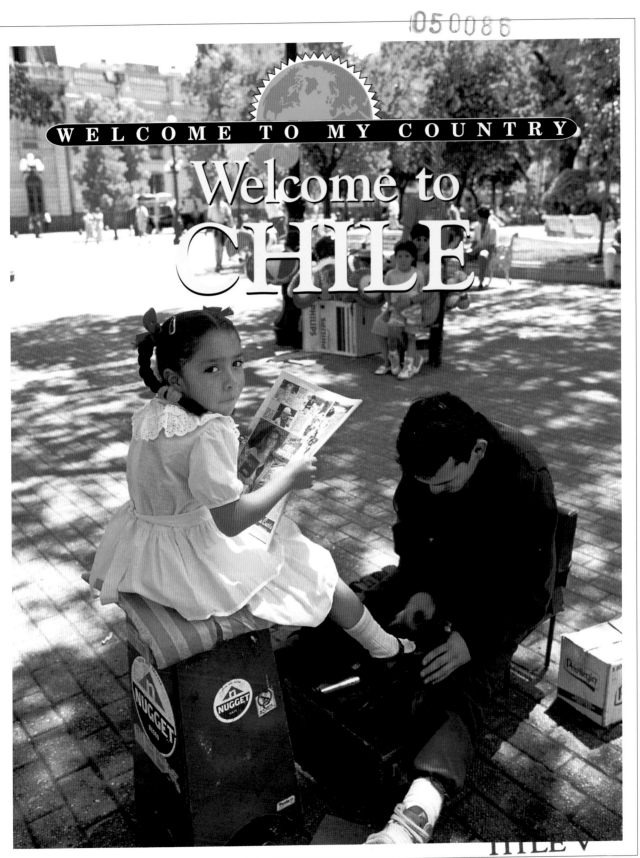

050086

WELCOME TO MY COUNTRY

Welcome to
CHILE

TITLE V
05.01 - 171

Gareth Stevens Publishing
A WORLD ALMANAC EDUCATION GROUP COMPANY

Written by
KAREN KWEK

Edited by
MELVIN NEO

Edited in USA by
JENETTE DONOVAN GUNTLY

Designed by
GEOSLYN LIM

Picture research by
SUSAN JANE MANUEL

First published in North America in 2004 by
Gareth Stevens Publishing
A World Almanac Education Group Company
330 West Olive Street, Suite 100
Milwaukee, Wisconsin 53212 USA

Please visit our web site at
www.garethstevens.com
For a free color catalog describing
Gareth Stevens Publishing's list of high-quality
books and multimedia programs,
call 1-800-542-2595 (USA) or
1-800-387-3178 (Canada)
Gareth Stevens Publishing fax: (414) 332-3567.

© **TIMES MEDIA PRIVATE LIMITED 2004**
Originated and designed by Times Editions
An imprint of Times Media Private Limited
A member of the Times Publishing Group
Times Centre, 1 New Industrial Road
Singapore 536196
http://www.timesone.com.sg/te

Library of Congress Cataloging-in-Publication Data
Kwek, Karen.
Welcome to Chile / Karen Kwek.
p. cm. — (Welcome to my country)
Summary: An overview of the geography, history,
government, economy, people, and culture of Chile.
Includes bibliographical references and index.
ISBN 0-8368-2558-6 (lib. bdg.)
1. Chile—Juvenile literature. [1. Chile.]
I. Title. II. Series.
F3058.5.K94   2004
983—dc22   2003059177

Printed in Singapore

1 2 3 4 5 6 7 8 9 08 07 06 05 04

PICTURE CREDITS
Jorge Acuña/International Bildarchive: 35
Agence France Presse: 14 (both), 29, 37
Art Directors & TRIP Photo Library:
    3 (center)
Victor Engelbert: 40
Focus Team — Italy: 6
Eduardo Gil: 1, 12, 15 (top), 23, 33 (bottom)
HBL Network Photo Agency: 38
Horst von Irmer/International Bildarchive:
    2, 3 (top), 4, 7, 8, 11, 16, 18, 21, 22,
    24, 25, 27, 28, 30, 31 (both), 34, 36,
    39, 41, 43, 45
Hutchison Library: 9, 33 (top)
South America Pictures: 17
Ricardo Carrasco Stuparchi: cover,
    3 (bottom), 13, 15 (bottom), 20, 26, 32
Maureille Vautier: 5, 10, 19

Digital Scanning by Superskill Graphics Pte Ltd

Contents

Words that appear in the glossary are printed in **boldface** type the first time they occur in the text.

Welcome to Chile!

Chile is a long, narrow country located in South America. Bordering Chile's east side is the longest mountain range in the world, the Andes. Chile is known for its **diverse** geography, from deserts to deep forests, and for its mixture of cultures. Let's meet the Chileans and explore their interesting land!

Opposite: This church in Chile's capital city, Santiago, was built during the years when the Spanish ruled the country.

Below: Scientists from around the world travel to study the statues found on Chile's Easter Island.

The Flag of Chile

The Chilean flag has three colors. Blue is for Chile's clear sky, white is for the snow on the Andes Mountains, and red is for the Chileans who died in the fight for **independence**. The white star is for the powers of the government.

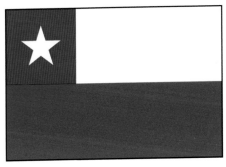

The Land

Chile touches the Pacific Ocean on its west side. The Andes mountain range separates Chile from Argentina and Bolivia. Thousands of islands along the coast, including Easter Island, are also part of Chile. The country covers about 292,182 square miles (756,751 square kilometers). Chile's highest mountain peak is Nevado Ojos del Salado, which stands 22,614 feet (6,893 meters) tall.

Left: Hikers often visit the Torres del Paine National Park in Chile to climb the park's massive **granite** mountains, which are millions of years old.

Left: The Atacama Desert is located in northern Chile. This desert is one of the driest places in the world.

Chile's land can be divided into three regions: the Andes mountain range, the central valley, and the coastal ranges.

The Andes mountain range is made up of **extinct** volcanoes and mountain peaks. The only land fit for farming is in the central valley. The area is also rich in minerals, such as **nitrates** and copper, which wash down to the central valley from the Andes range in rivers and streams. In the coastal ranges, the mountains are smaller and have flatter tops than in the Andes mountain range.

Climate

Because it is located south of the **equator**, Chile's seasons are opposite of those in North America. Summers last from December to March. Winters last from June to September.

Northern Chile is dry, with less than an inch of rain each year. In central Chile, seasons are mild. Summers are dry and warm, and winters are cool and rainy. Southern Chile's weather is cold and damp, and the area is often hit by storms and strong winds.

Left: Grapes grow well in the mild climate of central Chile. In the central valley, the mean temperature is 69° Fahrenheit (21° Celsius) in the summer and 48° F (9° C) in the winter.

Plants and Animals

Chile's northern deserts are so dry that only cacti and shrubs can grow. Central Chile has large forests of pine, southern beech, and eucalyptus trees. The giant **alerce**, the world's largest tree, grows in southern Chile.

Many unusual animals live in Chile, including the pudu, a species of deer, and the camel-like guanaco. Birds such as penguins, three types of flamingos, and Andean condors live in Chile. Sea lions, seals, and otters live on the coast.

Above: Alpacas live in the Andes mountain range. Like guanacos, alpacas are related to camels.

History

The Araucanians, a group of Native Americans, were the earliest people to live in what is now Chile. In the 1400s, the Incas, a group of Native Americans from Peru, invaded the country. The Incas **conquered** northern Chile, but the Araucanians were able to defend southern Chile from attack.

Left:
The bravery of the Araucanians in war has lead many Chileans to think of them as the country's first national heroes.

Left: This painting shows the Chilean and Spanish armies meeting in battle in 1817. The Chilean army was led by Bernardo O'Higgins. Today, many people consider O'Higgins to be the founding father of Chile.

Spanish Rule to Independence

Although Portuguese navigator Ferdinand Magellan was the first European to see Chile, the Spanish were the first Europeans to rule the country. Groups of Spanish explorers began to arrive in 1535. By 1541, the Spanish had founded the capital city of Santiago. The Spanish ruled Chile for more than three hundred years.

Chile declared independence from Spain in 1810, but the Spanish took back control in 1814. With help from Argentina, Bernardo O'Higgins won back Chile's independence in 1817.

Left: Bernardo O'Higgins (*center*) worked to bring peace and order to Chile, but his reforms angered many of Chile's **aristocrats**. In 1823, O'Higgins was forced to give up his position and leave Chile. He lived in Peru until his death in 1842.

A Struggling Young Nation

Bernardo O'Higgins served as Chile's head of state from 1817 to 1823. After he left office, the country's political groups fought for control. Between 1823 and 1830, there were as many as thirty changes in government. A new constitution and new leaders helped the country become more stable, and the economy improved. By the 1850s, many Chilean cities had begun to grow quickly. Large numbers of Chileans moved to the cities for a better quality of life and to find work.

War and Government Changes

From 1879 to 1883, Chile fought Peru and Bolivia in the War of the Pacific. At the same time, Chile's army fought groups of Araucanians all across the country. The Chilean army won both wars. In 1891, civil war broke out over who got to control Chile's minerals.

Chile's military ruled the country from 1924 to 1925, but the government quickly returned to **democracy**. In 1970, Salvador Allende Gossens was elected president of Chile, and the government became **socialist**.

Left:
While Salvador Allende Gossens was president of Chile, the prices of goods went up, and food was in short supply. Chileans began to protest, and in 1973, the president was forced out of office.

The Pinochet Government

In 1973, General Augusto Pinochet Ugarte led the attack against President Allende Gossens. Pinochet then became a **dictator**. His government tortured or killed Chileans who did not agree with his rules. Although it was harsh and cruel, Pinochet's government improved Chile's economy and trade.

In 1988, the Chileans voted to take Pinochet from power. Chile elected a new president, and in 1990, the country became democratic once again.

Above: Chilean president Ricardo Lagos Escobar (*left*) meets with Mireya Garcia (*right*), who represents a group of victims tortured by General Augusto Pinochet's forces. Several Chilean military leaders still support Pinochet. Others, including most government officials in Chile, feel that Pinochet is guilty of murder and other crimes.

Left: Many experts are still searching for the bodies of Chileans who have been missing since the rule of Pinochet. Chileans who were against Pinochet were often taken prisoner, and some were never heard from again.

Gabriela Mistral (1889–1957)

As a respected educator and writer, Gabriela Mistral traveled around the world to help reform libraries and schools. In 1945, she became the first Latin American woman to receive a Nobel Prize for Literature.

Gabriela Mistral

Claudio Arrau (1903–1991)

Chilean pianist Claudio Arrau was famous around the world. In 1967, upset by the political fighting in Chile, Arrau became a U.S. citizen. In 1984, he returned to Chile as a national hero.

Augusto Pinochet Ugarte (1915–)

From 1973 to 1990, Augusto Pinochet Ugarte ruled Chile. Experts believe he was responsible for the killing of many thousands of Chileans. In 1998, he was arrested in London and brought back to Chile on murder charges, but Chile's Supreme Court ruled that Pinochet was too ill to stand trial for his crimes.

Augusto Pinochet Ugarte

Government and the Economy

Today, Chile is a democratic country. The Chilean people elect their head of state, or president, to serve a six-year term. Chile's current president, Ricardo Lagos Escobar, was elected in 2000.

Each new Chilean president chooses his own **ministers**. The ministers are advisors to the president and serve six-year terms as part of the Cabinet.

Below:
Chile's National Congress building is located in the city of Valparaíso.

Chile's Lawmakers

The country's laws are made by the National Congress, which is made up of a Senate and a Chamber of Deputies.

Chile has forty-eight senators. Ten senators are chosen by the government, and the other thirty-eight senators are elected by the Chilean people. Chilean voters also choose all 120 members of the Chamber of Deputies.

In addition to the National Congress, Chile's Supreme Court, Constitutional Tribunal, and Security Council also help make decisions about laws.

The Economy

Since the early 1990s, Chile's economy has grown stronger. Many businesses from foreign countries have moved to Chile. The companies have created jobs and helped the Chilean economy.

Copper is Chile's largest **export**. In fact, Chile produces more copper than any other country in the world. Fish, chemicals, and wood are also essential Chilean exports.

Above: Chilean cities, such as La Serena, attract tourists from all over the globe. Tourism is growing and now plays an important role in Chile's economy.

Farming is very valuable to Chile's economy. Chilean farmers use modern machines that help produce food very quickly. Modern methods also help the farmers produce more food to sell.

Apples and grapes are two of Chile's main exports. Chile sells more fruit to other countries than any other nation in the world. Other exports include wheat, barley, lentils, and peas. The Chileans also raise livestock and export poultry and beef to countries such as Canada.

Left: These Chilean farmers are harvesting wheat. Later, the wheat will be processed at a mill.

People and Lifestyle

About three-fourths of Chileans are mestizos, or people who have both Europeans and Native Americans in their family **ancestry**. One-fifth of Chileans have Spanish, British, or German ancestry. A small number of Chileans are Native American.

Almost three-fourths of all Chileans, including Native Americans, live in central Chile because the farmland is good and the climate is mild. Many of them live in the area around Santiago.

Left: This group of Mapuche students and their teacher live in Temuco, in central Chile. The Mapuches are Araucanian Indians.

Rich and Poor

In Chile, there is a large gap between the lifestyles of the rich and the poor. Poor Chileans often live in run-down huts with dirt floors and no electricity or running water. On the other hand, wealthy Chileans often live in large, elegant houses with lush gardens. It is common to find expensive houses and broken-down shacks in the same city.

Above:
Wealthy Chileans often hire servants and gardeners to care for their large homes. People with European ancestry make up most of Chile's upper class. The middle class is made up mostly of mestizos, while the lower class is made up mainly of Native Americans, often of Mapuche ancestry.

Family Life

Families are very important in Chilean society. Once married, newlyweds start their own homes, but families often remain very close. Many grandparents, and even uncles and aunts, help care for children. In many Chilean families, both parents earn money and help run the household.

Chile is one of the few countries in the world that does not allow divorce. Many Chileans want this changed, so Chile's Senate is discussing the issue.

Above: Middle-class Chileans tend to have small families with only one or two children.

Women at Work

Since the early 1900s, many Chilean women have entered the **workforce**. This trend increased after 1973, when many men were fired from their jobs, were taken prisoner, or disappeared after protesting against the Pinochet government. Without the men in the household working, the women had to earn money to support their families. Women have gone on to become doctors, lawyers, and even senators.

Below: These Chilean women are working in a fish processing factory. Women in Chile work in many fields, but are often paid less than what a man is paid for doing the same job. Women in Chile are now fighting to end this **discrimination**.

Education

Chilean children attend primary school from ages six to fourteen. In the first four years, children study subjects such as math, history, art, and music. Later, they learn English, biology, and metal work. Students then go on to a four-year secondary school. For two years, they study general subjects. In the third year, students choose a social science, natural science, or **vocational** program.

Left:
Field trips in Chile, such as this one for a group of primary school students, help children learn outside of the classroom.

Higher Learning

After completing secondary school, some Chilean students go on to college. The country has both public and private colleges and universities. Students can study subjects such as math, business, engineering, economics, natural and social sciences, and religion. At some Chilean universities, students can also study **astronomy**. The country's oldest university, the University of Chile, was built in 1843 and is located in Santiago.

Above: The Catholic University of Chile, which is located in Santiago, is run by the Roman Catholic Church.

Religion

In Chile, people are free to practice any religion they choose. A large number of Chileans are Roman Catholic. Other Christian Chileans belong to Lutheran, Methodist, or Baptist churches. A small number of Chileans are Jewish.

Some Native Americans in Chile still practice the religion of their ancestors, shamanism. Shamanism teaches that spirits live in natural objects, such as rocks, trees, and rivers.

Below: Almost 90 percent of all Chileans belong to the Roman Catholic religion. Many of them attend mass regularly and go on religious retreats.

Roman Catholicism

The Spanish brought the Roman Catholic faith to Chile in the 1500s. Since then, Roman Catholicism has influenced many parts of Chilean life, including the country's works of art. Many paintings and sculptures in Chile use religious symbols and scenes.

The Roman Catholic Church also plays an important role in society by running many schools and hospitals.

Above:
President Lagos (*right*) meets the cardinal of Chile's Roman Catholic Church (*center*). A cardinal is a high-ranking leader in the church who is second in status only to the pope.

Language

Spanish is Chile's official language. It was brought to the country in the 1500s by settlers from Spain. Since then, the language has stayed almost the same, except for a few words the Chileans borrowed from the Native Americans.

Some Native Americans in Chile still speak their native languages, such as the Mapuche language, Mapudungun. The Aymara, from Chile, Peru, and Bolivia, speak the Aymaran language.

Left: The Chilean education system is serious about making sure all young Chileans can read. About 95 percent of all Chileans over age fifteen can read and write.

Literature

Chile has produced many fine writers and poets. Alonso de Ercilla y Zuniga was one of the country's first poets. He wrote *La Araucana*, a poem about the Araucanians and the Spanish. In 1862, Alberto Blest Gana (1830–1920) wrote the famous book *Martin Rivas*. Modern Chilean writers include José Donoso (1924–1996) and best-selling author Isabel Allende (1942–). In 1971, Pablo Neruda (1904–1973), Chile's best-known poet, was awarded the Nobel Prize for Literature.

Arts

Chile's artistic style has been inspired by Spanish and other European styles. The country's earliest artists often used religious themes in their work. Today, many artists in Chile choose subjects from everyday life.

Many Chilean artists, including Roberto Matta (1911–2002), are well known around the world. Matta painted in the surrealist style, combining colors and objects to create dreamlike images.

Below:
In 1908, the Museo Partenon, Chile's first art museum, opened in the city of Santiago. The museum, which is now called the Contemporary Art Museum of Santiago, houses works by artists from Chile and around the world.

Chilean artist Nemesio Antunez (1918–1993) used simple shapes to represent people and landscapes. Mario Toral (1934–) has become famous for his **murals**, which he paints on public buildings. Isabel Klotz (1962–) is one of Chile's best-known female artists.

In addition to fine artworks, Chileans make many crafts, too. They are known for their ceramics, knitted and woven cloth, and woven baskets.

Above: This bird sculpture is made of Chile's national stone, **lapis lazuli**.

Theater

In the 1930s, professors and students from the University of Chile founded the Teatro Experimental. It was one of the first theater companies to perform Chilean dramas. The company inspired play writers such as Armando Moock (1884–1942) to write about Chile's political and social issues.

Today, Chileans are able to enjoy a wide range of theater acts. The country holds several local and international theater festivals each year.

Left: The Municipal Theater in Santiago opened in 1857. Today, well-known ballet companies, opera groups, and orchestras from around the world perform there.

Music and Dance

Chilean folk music is often used to tell stories about Chile's history. Musicians sometimes play along on a *guitarron* (gee-tah-ROHN), which is a large bass guitar; a cactus rainstick, which sounds like rain; or a *bombo* (BOHM-boh), an ancient drum made from a tree stump.

Chile's national dance is the *cueca* (KWHEY-kah). The cueca is danced by male and female partners, and the steps become very lively.

Above: Violeta Parra (1917-1967), one of Chile's most gifted folksingers and songwriters, often wrote songs about poor people and Chilean workers.

Leisure

Chileans often enjoy leisure time by flying kites or going on picnics. Some people also surf or relax on the beaches of La Serena or Viña del Mar.

In cities, Chileans enjoy eating at restaurants or going to shopping malls. Chilean families like to visit parks, too. Parque Metropolitano, a popular park in Santiago, is a favorite spot for many families to walk or visit the zoo.

Left: Vendors sell colorful balloons, balls, and toys at Forest Park in the city of Santiago. Many Chilean families relax in city parks during weekends.

Games in Chile

Many Chilean men play *rayuela* (rah-yoo-EH-lah), a game originally from Spain. Players throw a heavy metal disc at a rope held above the ground. The goal of the game is to balance the metal disc on the rope.

Chilean children play rayuela, too, but they use coins instead of discs. They also spin tops or play familiar games such as hula hoop or hopscotch.

Above: *Chueca* (CHWEH-kah), which is similar to hockey, is an ancient Mapuche game. Players may only touch or pass the wooden ball with their curved wooden sticks. The aim is to hit the ball across the other team's goal line.

Sports

Horseback riding has been a traditional Chilean sport for centuries. Chileans and tourists often travel on horseback to see the country's diverse landscape. For daring horseback riders, being in a rodeo is popular. Each autumn, large numbers of Chileans turn out to watch the *huasos* (WAH-sohs), or Chilean cowboys, compete in a rodeo contest.

Chileans also go hiking, waterskiing, snow skiing, fishing, and scuba diving.

Above: In Chilean rodeo contests, the huasos do not use rope to round up the cattle. Instead, they use trained horses to guide the cattle into a pen.

Soccer and Other Sports

Many Chileans are fans of *fútbol* (foot-BOL), or soccer. In the 1962 FIFA World Cup, the Chilean team won third place. In the 2000 Olympic Games, Chile won a bronze medal. Today, Chilean players such as Ivan Zamorano and Marcelo Salas have become stars in international soccer.

Chile also has produced fine athletes in other sports, including automobile racing, swimming, running, and tennis.

Left:
Ivan Zamorano (*left*) is the current captain of Chile's national soccer team. In 2000, he led Chile's Olympic team and helped them to win the country's first medal in soccer.

Religious Holidays

Many holidays in Chile are religious. Semana Santa, or Holy Week, occurs in late March or early April and ends on Easter Sunday. During Holy Week, Chileans attend mass and pray. The festival of Cuasimodo follows Holy Week. Priests visit people who were too sick to attend church. A parade of people, including huasos, rides along.

Below: People on brightly decorated bicycles, carriages, and carts take part in Cuasimodo parades in towns and villages all over central Chile.

La Tirana

La Tirana is Chile's patron saint. A festival is held in her honor each year from July 12 to July 15. Legends say, long ago, a Native American woman grew to hate the Spanish after they killed her father. She began to kill any Spanish person who came near her or her people. For this, she was named *la tirana*, or "the **tyrant**." La Tirana later fell in love with a Spanish miner and became a Catholic to be with him.

Food

In Chile, breakfast is a light meal. The main meal of the day is lunch, which often includes a salad, a meat dish, and vegetables. In the afternoon, Chileans have tea with sandwiches, breads, and cakes. Dinner is usually just one dish.

Food in Chile is simple but tasty. Because the country borders an ocean, Chileans eat and sell a lot of seafood, including lobster, crab, and many kinds of fish. In fact, Chile sells more salmon than any other country except Norway.

Left: A variety of seafood dishes are popular in Chile, including clams topped with melted cheese and Chilean sea bass. Seafood is often served with Chilean wine.

Left: This woman is selling baked *empanadas* (ehm-pa-NAH-dahs), or stuffed pastries. Empanadas are a favorite Chilean snack and are often filled with chopped beef, eggs, onions, olives, and raisins.

During summer, many Chileans eat *cazuela* (kah-SWEH-lah), which is a soup made with rice, potato, and corn. Another common Chilean dish is steak covered with fried eggs and onions.

Humitas (oo-MEE-tahs) are a favorite Chilean snack. Humitas are made by filling corn husks with corn, fried onions, basil, salt, and pepper.

El completo (ehl kohm-PLEH-toh) is considered Chile's most popular dish. It is a hot dog covered with tomatoes, ketchup, mayonnaise, and **guacamole**.

PERU

BOLIVIA

BRAZIL

PARAGUAY

TARAPACÁ

• La Tirana

ANTOFAGASTA

Tropic of Capricorn

Atacama Desert

Loa

ATACAMA

Nevada Ojos del Salado
(22,614 ft/6,893 m)

A n d e s

EASTER ISLAND

La Serena •

COQUIMBO

Juan Fernández Islands

Viña del Mar •
Valparaíso

• **VALPARAÍSO**

SANTIAGO •
■ **REGIÓN METROPOLITANA (SANTIAGO)**

EL LIBERTADOR GENERAL BERNARDO O'HIGGINS

URUGUAY

MAULE

BÍO-BÍO

Concepcíon •

Bío-Bío

ARGENTINA

PACIFIC

OCEAN

Temuco •

LA ARAUCANÍA

Ranco Lake

Chacao Straits

Llanquihue Lake

LOS LAGOS

ATLANTIC

OCEAN

▬▬▬	National Boundary
───	Regional Boundary
■	Capital
•	City
～～	River

AISÉN DEL GENERAL CARLOS IBÁÑEZ DEL CAMPO

MAGELLANES Y DE LA ANTARCTICA CHILENA

Torres del Paine

Strait of Magellan

CHILE

Cape Horn

N

A B C D

1 2 3 4 5

Aisén del General
    Carlos Ibáñez del
    Campo (region)
    B4–B5
Andes B3–C1
Antofagasta
    (region) B1–C2
Argentina B5–D2
Atacama (region)
    B2–C2
Atacama Desert
    B1–B2
Atlantic Ocean
    C5–D2

Bío-Bío (region) B3
Bío-Bío (river) B3
Bolivia B1–D1
Brazil D1–D3

Cape Horn C5
Chacao Straits B4
Concepción B3
Coquimbo
    (region) B2

Easter Island A2
El Libertador
    General Bernardo
    O'Higgins
    (region) B3

Juan Fernández
    Islands A3

La Araucanía
    (region) B3
La Serena B2
La Tirana B1
Llanquihue Lake B4
Loa (river) B1–C1
Los Lagos
    (region) B4

Above: Grapes from Chile's central valley are used to make wine.

Magallanes y de
    la Antártica
    Chilena (region)
    B4–C5
Maule (region) B3

Nevado Ojos del
    Salado B2–C2

Pacific Ocean
    A1–B5
Paraguay C1–D2
Peru B1

Ranco Lake B3
Región
    Metropolitana
    (Santiago)
    (region) B3

Santiago B3
Strait of Magellan
    B5–C5

Tarapacá (region)
    B1–C1
Temuco B3
Torres del Paine B5

Uruguay D2–D3

Valparaíso (city) B3
Valparaíso (region)
    B2–B3
Viña del Mar B3

Quick Facts

Official Name   Republic of Chile

Capital   Santiago

Official Language   Spanish

Population   15,498,930 (July 2002 estimate)

Land Area   292,182 square miles (756,751 square km)

Regions   Aisén del General Carlos Ibáñez del Campo, Antofagasta, La Araucanía, Atacama, Bío-Bío, Coquimbo, El Libertador General Bernardo O'Higgins, Los Lagos, Magallanes y de la Antártica Chilena, Maule, Región Metropolitana (Santiago), Tarapacá, Valparaíso

Major Cities   Concepción, Santiago, Valparaíso, Viña del Mar

Highest Point   Nevado Ojos del Salado 22,614 feet (6,893 m)

Major Rivers   Bío-Bío, Loa

Main Religions   Roman Catholicism, Protestantism

Major Holidays   Semana Santa (late March or early April), La Tirana (July 12–July 15), National Unity Day (first Monday of September), Independence Day (September 18)

Currency   Chilean peso (716 CLP = U.S. $1 as of 2003)

Opposite: The views from Easter Island's coast attract tourists from around the world.

Glossary

alerce: a type of giant cypress tree that grows in Chile and Argentina.

ancestry: a direct line of family members from the past, farther back than grandparents.

aristocrats: members of a country's upper class who usually come from royal or noble families.

astronomy: the study of objects outside of Earth's atmosphere, such as stars and planets.

conquered: invaded and took over a land using force.

democracy: a government in which the country's citizens can lead and can elect leaders by vote.

dictator: a ruler who has complete authority over a country.

discrimination: the practice of treating a person or a group less fairly than other people or groups.

diverse: made up of many different parts or of different qualities.

equator: an imaginary line around the middle of the earth, an equal distance from both the North and South Poles.

export (n): a product sent out of a country to be sold in another country.

extinct: no longer active.

guacamole: mashed avocado mixed with spices and seasonings.

granite: a very hard rock that stands up to the weather for millions of years without breaking down hardly at all.

independence: the state of being free from control by others.

lapis lazuli: a blue stone that is found only in Chile and Afghanistan.

ministers: high government officials who advise the president and who are in charge of parts of the government.

murals: large pictures painted directly onto walls or ceilings.

nitrates: a type of mineral salt often used as a fertilizer or to preserve meat.

socialist: a person or group that believes the government should own all property and should control the country's economy.

tyrant: someone who obeys no laws and who is often harsh or cruel.

vocational: related to an occupation, profession, or skilled trade.

workforce: the people in a country who work, most often outside the home.

More Books to Read

Chile. Enchantment of the World second series. Sylvia McNair (Children's Book Press)

Chile. First Reports Countries series. Cynthia Fitterer Klingel and Robert B. Noyed (Compass Point Books)

Chile. Festivals of the World series. Susan Roraff (Gareth Stevens)

Easter Island: Giant Stone Statues Tell of a Rich and Tragic Past. Caroline Arnold (Houghton Mifflin)

Folk Tales from Chile. Brenda Hughes (Hippocrene Books, Inc.)

Hats on for Polka Dot. Kathleen Sampson (The Robin Company Press)

Land of the Wild Llama: A Story of the Patagonian Andes. Audrey Fraggalosch (Soundprints)

Mariana and the Merchild: A Folk Tale from Chile. Caroline Pitcher (Wm. B. Eerdmans Publishing Co.)

Tierra Del Fuego: A Journey to the End of the Earth. Peter Lourie (Boyds Mills Press)

Videos

My Family from Chile. Families Around the World series. (Schlessinger Media)

Treasures of the Andes. Nature series. (PBS)

Web Sites

flagspot.net/flags/cl.html

www.alpacainfo.com

www.extremescience.com/DriestPlace.htm

www.mapzones.com/world/south_america/ chile_and_easter_island/

www.pbs.org/wgbh/nova/lostempires/ easter

www.worldatlas.com/webimage/ countrys/samerica/cl.htm

Due to the dynamic nature of the Internet, some web sites stay current longer than others. To find additional web sites, use a reliable search engine with one or more of the following keywords to help you locate information about Chile. Keywords: *alerce, Isabel Allende, Atacama, Easter Island, Bernardo O'Higgins, Santiago.*

Index